Casting the Runes

A Tale of Cursed Knowledge and
Deadly Supernatural Forces

A Modern Translation

Adapted for the Contemporary Reader

M.R. James

Translated by Tim Zengerink

Table of Contents

i

Preface - Message to the Reader

What If You Could Help Rebuild the Greatest Library in Human History?

Thousands of years ago, the Library of Alexandria stood as the crown jewel of human achievement — a sanctuary where the collected wisdom of every known civilization was gathered, preserved, and shared freely.

And then, it was lost.

Through fire, conquest, and the slow erosion of time, humanity lost not just books — but ideas, dreams, discoveries, and stories that could have changed the world forever.

Today, the Library of Alexandria lives again — and you are invited to be a part of its restoration.

Our mission is simple yet profound:

To rebuild the greatest library the world has ever known, and to translate all timeless works into every language and dialect, so that no seeker of knowledge is ever left behind again.

By joining our movement to rebuild the modern Library of Alexandria, you become part of an unprecedented mission:

- **Unlimited Access to the Greatest Audiobooks & eBooks Ever Written:**

  Instantly explore thousands of legendary works—Plato, Shakespeare, Jane Austen, Leo Tolstoy, and countless more. All instantly available to read or listen, placing a complete literary universe at your fingertips.

- **Beautiful Paperback & Deluxe Editions at Printing Cost**

  Own any title as an elegant paperback, deluxe hardcover, or stunning collectible boxset—offered to you at true printing cost, delivered straight to your door. Build your personal Library of Alexandria, crafted for beauty, built for durability, and worthy of proud display.

- **Fresh Translations for Modern Readers—in Every Language & Dialect**

  Enjoy timeless masterpieces reimagined in clear, contemporary language—no more outdated phrases or obscure references. Alongside the original versions, we're tirelessly translating these classics into every language and dialect imaginable, ensuring accessibility and understanding across cultures and generations.

- **Join a Global Renaissance of Literature & Knowledge**

  You directly support expanding our library, publishing deluxe editions at true cost, translating works into all global languages, and bringing humanity's greatest stories to people everywhere. By joining today, you're not just preserving a legacy of masterpieces; you set in motion a powerful wave of literary accessibility.

Become a Torchbearer of Knowledge.

Join us for free now at **LibraryofAlexandria.com**

Together, we will ensure that the light of human wisdom never fades again.

With gratitude and a shared love of knowledge,

The Modern Library of Alexandria Team

Visit:

www.libraryofalexandria.com

Or scan the code below:

Introduction

The Scholar's Curse
and the Mechanics of Supernatural Doom

Among all of M.R. James's ghost stories, Casting the Runes stands out as one of the most suspenseful, structurally complete, and cinematically influential tales in his entire body of work. First published in 1911 in More Ghost Stories of an Antiquary, it blends the antiquarian flavor and restrained horror James is best known for with a more dynamic narrative—one filled with pursuit, detection, and confrontation. In this story, we move beyond passive observation into the realm of active threat: the protagonist is not merely haunted by a ghost or troubled by an uncanny object; he is cursed, deliberately and maliciously, by a living antagonist who wields dark power through ancient runic symbols.

This tale presents a unique hybrid of the Jamesian form. It retains the familiar trappings of dusty archives, skeptical academics, and folkloric relics, yet it overlays these elements with a tight thriller plot. Casting the Runes is, in essence, a supernatural revenge story, a modernized tale of black magic that trades in intellectual snobbery, invisible forces, and the slow ticking of an unseen clock counting down to death. It is a story of transfer, of displacement, of cursed knowledge passed along like a fatal contagion.

The narrative centers on Edward Dunning, a scholarly critic who anonymously rejects a paper submitted to an academic society by Mr. Karswell, a mysterious and dangerous occultist. In retaliation, Karswell "casts the runes" on Dunning—a subtle, secret act that begins an unstoppable countdown to his death unless the curse is returned. What follows is a cat-and-mouse game between the rational and the arcane, as Dunning scrambles to identify the danger, comprehend its mechanics, and, ultimately, find a way to survive.

This introduction will unpack the intricacies and implications of Casting the Runes, exploring its structure, characters, thematic richness, and broader literary influence. We will analyze how James constructs a world in which ancient evil thrives in plain sight, hidden beneath the trappings of polite society and modern scholarship. We'll explore the story's innovations—its depiction of a living villain, its subtle use of procedural plotting, and its terrifying suggestion that the supernatural, when systematized, can become as methodical and lethal as science itself. More than a ghost story, Casting the Runes is a supernatural thriller with philosophical weight, one that forces us to ask what happens when forbidden knowledge is wielded by those who understand it—and what chance we stand if we are the targets.

Karswell, Dunning, and the Battle Between the Seen and the Hidden

One of the most remarkable aspects of Casting the Runes is its antagonist. Mr. Karswell is not a ghost, demon, or shadowy remnant of a cursed past. He is very much alive—and terrifyingly effective. As an occultist with genuine supernatural power, Karswell is both a satirical figure and a serious threat. He embodies a specific anxiety of the Edwardian age: the intersection of arcane knowledge and modern capability. He's the kind of man who can entertain children with fireworks and illusions, yet also conjure malevolent forces using ancient symbols and secret texts.

Karswell's danger lies not just in his command of forbidden lore, but in his ability to weaponize it with precision. The act of "casting the runes" involves inscribing runic symbols onto a piece of paper, which must then be secretly passed to the victim. Once this occurs, the countdown begins: strange occurrences, oppressive dreams, and eventually death at the hands of an unseen creature. What makes this form of magic so frightening is its anonymity and precision—it is a spell of exact rules and quiet execution, not chaotic sorcery.

In contrast, Edward Dunning is an intellectual everyman. A scholar of ancient texts, he is rational, urbane, and deeply unprepared for the forces arrayed against him. His first encounters with the supernatural are subtle: a whisper in a library, a dark presence following him, dreams of pursuit. James excels at using these light touches to unsettle the reader, slowly shifting the tone from detached analysis to full-fledged dread.

As Dunning uncovers the truth, aided by the brother of a previous victim, the story takes on the feel of a supernatural detective narrative. There are clues to uncover, documents to decipher, and a clear time limit. The tension lies not in whether the supernatural is real—it clearly is—but in whether Dunning can escape it. This structural twist gives Casting the Runes a uniquely modern momentum among James's stories.

What makes Karswell especially terrifying is his anonymity. He doesn't make threats. He doesn't confront his enemies. He simply chooses them, curses them, and walks away. His power, once set in motion, does not require his presence. He is the perfect supernatural antagonist for a modern world—remote, calculating, and dangerously understated. His victims often don't even know they're being targeted until it's too late.

The Curse as Technology: Systematizing the Supernatural

Unlike the ghostly phenomena in many of James's other stories, which are ambiguous or poetic, the threat in Casting the Runes is methodical and almost scientific. The curse is not simply the result of a haunted object or a buried crime—it is a transmittable force, akin to a virus or a bomb, activated by the mere presence of a runic slip of paper. This introduces a terrifying logic to the supernatural: a system that can be learned, deployed, and evaded—but only if you understand its rules.

In this way, the story anticipates the structure of much later horror media, especially in the 20th and 21st centuries. From cursed videotapes in The Ring to viral hauntings in It Follows, the idea that the supernatural operates according to hidden rules has become a staple of modern horror. And Casting the Runes is perhaps one of the earliest stories to articulate this idea with such precision.

The narrative hinges on the act of reversal. Dunning's only hope of survival is to return the runes to Karswell without his knowledge, thus transferring the curse back to its originator. This final act plays out with exquisite tension: a train journey, a dropped envelope, a moment of distraction, and the horrifying suggestion that Karswell is aware—but too late to stop it. The ending is subtle but chilling. Karswell dies in an "accident"—attacked by a spectral beast that tears him apart. The implication is clear: justice has been served, but only through cleverness and desperation.

This "passing of the curse" structure gives the story a moral complexity. The supernatural is not omniscient—it is programmed. It doesn't punish evil; it punishes whoever holds the runes. And that means the true horror is not just the curse itself, but the randomness and vulnerability it implies. Knowledge offers no protection. Innocence is irrelevant. You live only if you're clever enough to escape.

James's decision to mechanize the supernatural does not make it less frightening—it makes it more so. He shows us a world where the ancient and arcane can intersect with the modern and mundane, creating a new kind of terror: impersonal, inevitable, and invisible until it is too late.

Literary Influence, Adaptations, and Enduring Legacy

Casting the Runes has enjoyed a long and influential afterlife, particularly in visual media. The most famous adaptation is Jacques Tourneur's 1957 film Night of the Demon (also known as Curse of the Demon), a masterfully crafted horror film that brings the story into a Cold War-era setting. Though the film alters some plot details and shows the demon explicitly—something James would likely have abhorred—it captures the essence of the story: the idea of a modern man hunted by ancient forces, and the race against time to undo a mystical death sentence.

The story's core themes have echoed through countless works in horror fiction and film. The idea of cursed objects that must be passed along or returned, of time-limited hauntings, and of the supernatural as a procedural force, all trace their lineage to this deceptively quiet story. Even the structure of supernatural thrillers—combining detective work with occult mystery—owes much to James's innovations here.

More than any other of James's works, Casting the Runes also elevates the ghost story into something broader: a tale of confrontation between the visible and the hidden, between knowledge and fear. It is not merely about being haunted; it is about being targeted. It is about the terror of realizing that someone— somewhere—has already doomed you, and you don't even know how or when it will arrive.

And in this realization, James touches something profoundly modern. In a world of invisible threats, bureaucratic violence, and systems too complex to understand, Casting the Runes remains deeply relevant. It reminds us that fear is not always loud. Sometimes it is a piece of paper, passed in silence. A symbol tucked in your pocket. A whisper in the dark.

And once it finds you, it will not stop.

Unless you find a way to give it back.

Casting the Runes

April 15, 190–

Dear Sir,

The Council of the —— Association has asked me to return the draft of your paper, The Truth of Alchemy, which you offered to present at our upcoming meeting. I'm writing to let you know that the Council has decided not to include it in the program.

Sincerely,

——, Secretary

April 18

Dear Sir,

I regret to inform you that I am too busy to meet with you to discuss your proposed paper. Also, our rules don't allow for the matter to be discussed with a Committee of the Council, as you suggested. Please know that your paper was given full consideration and was reviewed by someone very qualified. It was not rejected for personal reasons in any way.

Sincerely,

_____

April 20

The Secretary of the —— Association respectfully informs Mr. Karswell that it is not possible to share the name(s) of the person or people who reviewed his paper. The Secretary also wishes to say that he will not be replying to any more letters on this matter.

***

"Who is Mr. Karswell?" asked the Secretary's wife. She had dropped by his office and, maybe without meaning to snoop, picked up the last of three letters that had just been brought in.

"Well, right now, he's a very angry man," her husband replied. "But honestly, I don't know much about him. He's rich, lives at a place called Lufford Abbey in Warwickshire, and he claims to be an alchemist. He wants to share his ideas with us—but that's really all I know. Other than that, I definitely don't want to see him anytime soon. Now, if you're ready, shall we go?"

"What did you do to upset him?" she asked.

"The usual thing. He sent us a paper he wanted to present at the next meeting. We gave it to Edward Dunning to review—he's one of the few people who actually understands that sort of thing—and Dunning said it was complete nonsense. So, we turned it down. Since then, Karswell's been sending me angry letters. The latest one was demanding to know who reviewed his paper. You saw how I answered. Just don't tell anyone about it, please."

"Of course not. I'd never do that. But I do hope he doesn't find out it was poor Mr. Dunning."

"Poor Mr. Dunning? Why call him that? He's perfectly fine—lots of hobbies, a comfortable house, and plenty of free time."

"I just meant I'd feel sorry for him if Karswell found out and started bothering him."

"Ah, yes. In that case, you're right. He would be poor Mr. Dunning then."

***

The Secretary and his wife were out having lunch with friends who were from Warwickshire. Mrs. Secretary had already planned to ask them about Mr. Karswell, but she didn't have to bring it up herself. The hostess turned to her husband and said, "I saw the Abbot of Lufford this morning."

He raised his eyebrows. "Really? What's he doing in London?"

"No idea. He was coming out of the British Museum when I drove by."

Naturally, Mrs. Secretary asked if this was a real abbot.

"Oh no," the woman replied. "He's just someone who bought Lufford Abbey a few years ago. His real name is Karswell."

"Is he a friend of yours?" asked Mr. Secretary, giving his wife a quick wink.

That one question opened the floodgates. The hosts had nothing good to say about Mr. Karswell. No one really knew what he did with his time. His staff were rude and creepy. He'd made up his own religion, and no one could figure out what weird things he did in private. He got offended easily and held grudges forever. He had a frightening face (at least according to the hostess—her husband wasn't quite sure about that), never did anything kind, and whatever influence he had was always for the worse.

"Be fair now," the husband cut in. "Don't forget the treat he gave the school kids."

"Forget? I'm glad you brought it up! That's exactly the kind of man he is. Florence, listen to this: the first winter he moved into Lufford Abbey, he wrote to the local vicar and offered to show the school children some magic-lantern slides. He said he had new ones he thought they'd like. The vicar was surprised—Karswell had already complained about the children for playing near his property—but of course he agreed, and the event was scheduled. My husband went along to make sure everything was fine. Luckily, our own kids were at a party at our house that night, thank goodness.

"Because it turned out Mr. Karswell wanted to scare those kids half to death. He started with slides that weren't too bad—like Little Red Riding Hood—but even then, the wolf was so terrifying that a few of the younger children had to be taken out. Mr. Farrer said Karswell began by making this horrible howling sound like a wolf in the distance. It was the creepiest thing he'd ever heard. And the slides were amazingly realistic—too realistic. Nobody knew where he got them.

"The stories kept getting scarier. The kids were frozen in their seats, too scared to move. Then came a series of pictures showing a little boy walking through

Lufford Park in the evening—every kid there recognized the place. A creepy white figure started following him, then chasing him, and finally caught him. Whether it tore him apart or made him disappear, no one could tell. But the creature was terrifying—hopping and inhuman.

"Farrer said it gave him the worst nightmare of his life. Just imagine what it did to the children! He stopped the show and told Karswell it couldn't go on. But Karswell just said, 'Oh, you think it's time to end our little show and send them to bed? Very well!' Then he showed a final slide full of snakes, centipedes, and winged bugs, and somehow it looked like they were crawling out of the picture toward the kids. He even played a sound like dry rustling that made the kids scream and panic. Many were hurt trying to get out of the room, and I doubt a single one slept that night.

"There was a huge uproar in the village. The mothers blamed poor Mr. Farrer, and if the fathers could've gotten through Karswell's gates, I bet they'd have smashed every window in Lufford Abbey. So that's Mr. Karswell—the 'Abbot of Lufford.' You can see why we're not exactly excited to spend time with him."

"Yes," said the host. "Karswell seems like someone who could turn into a very dangerous man. I'd feel sorry for anyone who made him mad."

"Is he the one," said the Secretary, frowning in thought, "who wrote a History of Witchcraft about ten years ago? Or am I confusing him with someone else?"

"That's the one. Do you remember the reviews?"

"Absolutely. And more importantly, I knew the guy who wrote the most brutal review. So did you—John Harrington. He was at St. John's when we were."

"Oh yes, I remember him well. But I don't think I saw or heard anything from him again until I read about his inquest in the paper."

"Inquest?" one of the women asked. "What happened to him?"

"Well," said the host, "he fell out of a tree and broke his neck. But the weird part is why he was in the tree at all. It didn't make sense. He wasn't the type to do anything risky or strange. He was just walking home on a quiet country road one night—no one else around, no sign of danger. People in town liked him. Then all of a sudden, he starts running like crazy, drops his hat and walking stick, and climbs up a tree by the side of the road. It wasn't an easy tree to climb either. One of the branches broke, and he fell and died. When they found him the next morning, the look on his face was horrifying—like he had died from pure fear.

"People guessed he was being chased by something. Some said it might've been a wild dog or some animal that got loose, but there was no real proof. This happened back in 1889. I think his brother Henry— who I knew at Cambridge—is still trying to figure out what really happened. He believes someone wanted to hurt him, but honestly, I don't see how that explains it."

After a while, they started talking about the History of Witchcraft again.

"Did you ever read it?" the host asked.

"Yes, I did," said the Secretary. "I actually read the whole thing."

"Was it really that bad?"

"As far as writing goes, it was terrible. It deserved all the bad reviews. But worse than that, the book felt evil. The guy who wrote it believed every word, and I wouldn't be surprised if he actually tried some of the spells he wrote about."

"I only remember Harrington's review," said the host. "If I were the author, that would've ended my writing career for good. I'd be too embarrassed to write again."

"Well, it clearly didn't stop Karswell. Anyway, it's already 3:30—I've got to get going."

As they walked home, the Secretary's wife said, "I really hope that creepy man never finds out Mr. Dunning was the one who rejected his paper."

"I don't think he will," said the Secretary. "Dunning won't tell anyone—he knows it's private. And we won't either. Karswell doesn't even know his name, because Dunning hasn't published anything on that subject yet. The only risk is if Karswell asks the staff at the British Museum who's been reading about alchemy. But I can't exactly tell them not to talk about Dunning—that would just make them suspicious. Let's just hope the idea doesn't occur to him."

But Mr. Karswell was a smart man.

***

That's the background of the story.

One evening later that same week, Mr. Edward Dunning was on his way home from the British Museum, where he had been doing research. He lived alone in a cozy house in the suburbs, looked after by two kind women who had worked for him for many years.

There's not much more to say about what he looked like—we already know enough. Let's follow him now as he walks calmly and quietly home.

***

Mr. Edward Dunning took a train that got him within a couple of miles of his home. Then he rode an electric tram that dropped him about 300 yards from his front door. When he got on the tram, he was too tired to keep reading, and the lighting wasn't good anyway. Instead, he stared at the usual ads printed on the glass windows. He'd seen most of them before and barely noticed them anymore—except for one in the far corner that seemed unfamiliar.

The ad was written in blue letters on a yellow background. From where he sat, he could only make out a name—John Harrington—and possibly a date. Even though it didn't seem important, he was curious enough to move closer to read it more clearly. He was a little surprised. This ad was different. It said:

"In memory of John Harrington, F.S.A., of The Laurels, Ashbrooke. Died Sept. 18th, 1889. Three months were allowed."

The tram came to a stop. Dunning, still staring at the ad, didn't move until the conductor called out to him. "Sorry," he said. "I was looking at that ad—it's really strange, isn't it?" The conductor read it slowly. "Well, I've never seen that one before. That's weird. Somebody must be playing a joke," he said. He pulled out a cloth and wiped the window, even using a little spit. "Nope," he said, checking from outside. "That's not a sticker. It looks like it's actually part of the glass. What do you think, sir?"

Dunning rubbed the window with his glove and agreed—it really did seem like the writing was inside the glass. "Who handles the ads on these trams?" he asked. "Could you find out? I'd like to write down what it says."

Just then the driver called, "Let's go, George— time's up!" George replied, "Hang on—there's something odd going on up here. Come take a look at this glass." "What's wrong with the glass?" the driver asked as he came closer. "Who's Harrington? What is this all about?"

Dunning said, "I was just asking who's in charge of the tram ads. I think someone should look into this one."

"That's done at the company office," said the driver. "I think Mr. Timms handles that. When we park for the night, I'll leave a message. Maybe I'll have some answers tomorrow if you're riding again."

That ended the conversation for the night. Dunning later looked up Ashbrooke and found it was a place in Warwickshire.

The next day, he took the tram again—it was the same car—but it was too crowded to talk to the conductor. He did notice that the odd ad was gone.

That evening, back at home working in his study, one of his maids came in and told him two men from the tram company were at the door and eager to speak with him. He had almost forgotten about the ad, but he invited them in. It was the same conductor and driver. After giving them something to drink, Dunning asked what Mr. Timms had said.

"Well," said the conductor, "that's why we came by. Mr. Timms yelled at William here. He said there was no record of any ad like that—not ordered, not approved, not paid for, and definitely not installed. He told us we were wasting his time. I said, 'Then just come see it for yourself.' He agreed, and we went straight to the tram. I swear to you, that ad—with 'Harrington' in blue letters on yellow glass—was right there, like we both saw. You even helped me check it. Remember, I wiped the glass."

"I remember clearly," Dunning said. "So, what happened?"

"Well, it was gone," said the conductor. "And not broken or anything. The glass looked normal—no letters, no marks. I've never seen anything like it. You can ask William—he saw it too. But what's the point in me going on about it?"

"What did Mr. Timms say?" asked Dunning.

"He called us all sorts of names," the conductor admitted, "and honestly, I don't blame him. But William and I remembered that you had written it down, so we came to ask—could you please come talk to Mr. Timms and show him your note?"

"That's exactly what I told him," said William. "Go to a proper gentleman who'll speak up for us. Now maybe you'll believe me, George."

"Alright, alright," George said. "You didn't have to drag me here—I came on my own, didn't I? Still, we shouldn't be bothering you, sir, but if you could just stop by the office in the morning and explain what you saw, we'd be really grateful. It's not just about being called names—we're worried they'll think we made the whole thing up. And once they believe that, who knows what could happen to us?"

After more of the same, George and William thanked him and left.

Mr. Timms, who knew Mr. Dunning just a little, changed his mind the next day after hearing what Dunning had seen and being shown some proof. Because of that, William and George didn't get in trouble at work—but no one could explain what had happened.

Mr. Dunning stayed curious because of something that happened the next afternoon. He was walking from his club to catch his train when he saw a man up ahead handing out flyers. It wasn't a busy street, and Dunning didn't see him give a flyer to anyone else. As Dunning walked by, the man handed him one. Their hands touched for a moment, and Dunning felt a strange shock. The hand felt oddly rough and hot. He looked quickly at the man, but couldn't make out his face clearly, and later, no matter how hard he tried, he couldn't remember what the man looked like.

Dunning glanced at the flyer. It was blue, and in big letters, he saw the name "Harrington." Surprised, he reached for his glasses to read more, but just then, someone walking past snatched the paper from his hand and disappeared. Dunning looked around, but both the person who took the flyer and the man handing them out were gone.

The next day, Dunning went to the British Museum's Manuscript Room to do some research. As he set up his work, he thought he heard someone whisper his name behind him. He turned around quickly and knocked some papers off the desk. No one familiar was there except one of the staff, who nodded at him. Dunning picked up the papers, thinking he had them all, but then a heavy-set man behind him tapped his shoulder and handed him a missing piece. "Thanks," Dunning said, and the man left.

Later, Dunning asked the staff member who the man was. "That's Mr. Karswell," he said. "He asked me last week who the top experts on alchemy were, and I told him you were the best. I think he wants to meet you."

"Please, don't let that happen," Dunning replied quickly. "I really want to avoid him."

"No problem," said the staff member. "He doesn't come often. You probably won't run into him again."

Still, Dunning couldn't shake the uneasy feeling as he went home. Something felt off—like he was no longer just living his normal life, but was somehow being watched or followed. On the train and the tram, he sat close to others, wanting company, but both were nearly empty. The tram conductor, George, seemed distracted, busy counting passengers.

When Dunning got home, he found his doctor waiting. "Sorry to mess up your day, Dunning," the doctor said. "Your housekeepers are both very sick. I had to send them to the nursing home."

"What happened?" Dunning asked.

"Looks like food poisoning," said the doctor. "They said they bought shellfish from a street seller during dinner. But no one else in the neighborhood saw a seller. It's strange."

"Will they be okay?"

"They should be, but they won't be home for a while. Come dine at my house tonight and we'll sort everything out."

So Dunning didn't have to spend the evening alone, but it came with worry and inconvenience. The doctor, who had only recently moved to the area, was friendly, and dinner went fine. But when Dunning returned home around 11:30, the rest of the night was awful.

He got ready for bed and turned off the light. While lying there, he wondered if the charwoman would come early enough to bring him hot water. Suddenly, he heard the door to his study open. No footsteps followed, but he had made sure to close that door earlier. Embarrassed more than brave, he crept into the hallway in his nightgown and leaned over the railing to listen. There was no light, no more noise—just a sudden burst of hot air against his legs. He hurried back to his room and locked the door.

But things got worse. The lights weren't working. Maybe the power was cut, or something was wrong with the meter. He reached under his pillow for matches, but instead of matches, his hand touched something—a mouth, with teeth and hair. And he was sure it wasn't human. He panicked and ran to a spare room, locked the door, and sat with his ear against it, waiting for something to try to get in. But nothing did.

The next morning, Dunning slowly checked his room. The door was open, the window blinds were up, and everything seemed normal. His watch was in the right place. The only odd thing was the wardrobe door had swung open again, as it often did. Just then, the charwoman rang the back doorbell. He let her in and continued searching the house, but found nothing strange.

The rest of the day was gloomy. He didn't dare return to the Museum—Karswell might be there. His house felt creepy, and he didn't want to keep bothering the doctor. He visited the nursing home to check on his housekeepers, and their recovery made him feel a little better. At lunch, he went to his club and saw the Secretary of the Association, which lifted his spirits a bit. He told the Secretary about his sick servants and other simple things but didn't mention what was really bothering him.

"You've had a rough time," said the Secretary. "Come stay with us—we've got room and you need the company. Send your things over this afternoon."

Dunning didn't argue. As the day went on, he became more and more afraid of spending another night alone. He was almost happy to head home and pack.

When he arrived at his friend's home, they were surprised by how worn-out and anxious he looked. They did their best to help him feel normal again. But later that night, while he and the other man, Gayton, were smoking and chatting, Dunning grew quiet again.

Suddenly he said, "Gayton, I think that alchemist guy knows I was the one who got his paper rejected."

Gayton raised his eyebrows. "Why do you think that?"

Dunning explained what the Museum assistant had told him. Gayton agreed—it sounded likely. "Not that I'm worried," Dunning added, "but it would be a problem if I ran into him. I think he's dangerous."

They both sat quietly for a bit. Gayton noticed just how nervous and downcast Dunning had become. Finally, after hesitating, he asked, "Is something seriously bothering you?"

Dunning looked relieved. "Yes. I've been dying to talk about it. Do you know anything about a man named John Harrington?"

Gayton was startled and asked why.

Then Dunning told him everything—what had happened on the tram, at home, on the street—and how he felt haunted and afraid. When he finished, Gayton didn't know what to say.

He wondered whether to tell Dunning how Harrington had died. It was a terrible story, and Dunning was already clearly shaken. But Gayton also wondered if Karswell was somehow connected to both Dunning and Harrington. It was hard for a man of science like Gayton to believe, but maybe there was some sort of psychological trick being used—hypnosis or suggestion.

In the end, Gayton decided not to say too much yet. "I knew Harrington from Cambridge," he said, "and I think he died suddenly in 1889." He gave a few details about Harrington's work.

Later that night, Gayton talked it over with his wife. She immediately came to the conclusion he'd been considering all along: Karswell might be behind this. She reminded him that Harrington had a surviving brother named Henry, and suggested they try to contact him through some mutual friends from the day before.

Gayton said, "What if the brother is a total weirdo?"

"We can ask the Bennetts," his wife replied. "They know him." And she promised to talk to them the next day.

***

There's no need to explain exactly how Henry Harrington and Dunning ended up meeting.

***

The next important moment was a conversation between Dunning and Harrington. Dunning had told Harrington how his brother's name had strangely come up in his life, and he also shared some of the strange things that had happened to him afterward. Then

Dunning asked Harrington if he would be willing to talk about anything related to his brother's death.

Harrington was surprised, as you might expect, but he quickly agreed.

"John definitely wasn't acting like himself," he said. "There were several weeks, though not right before his death, when he seemed very uneasy. He had this idea that someone was following him. He wasn't the kind of person to imagine things, so it really stood out. I still believe someone was trying to harm him. And what you've told me about your own experience reminds me of what John went through. Do you think there could be a connection?"

"I've had a thought," Dunning said. "I heard your brother wrote a very harsh review of a book before he died. Recently, I've had a run-in with the man who wrote that book—and I think he took it personally."

"Wait," Harrington said. "Was his name Karswell?"

"That's the one."

Harrington leaned back in his chair. "Then that settles it for me. I need to explain more. From some things my brother said, I'm pretty sure he was starting to believe—though he didn't want to—that Karswell was behind his troubles. There's something else that might be important too. John loved music and often went to concerts in the city. About three months before he died, he went to one and gave me the program afterward. He told me, 'I almost lost this one—I must've dropped it and was searching under my seat. Then the man next to me offered me his, said he didn't need it anymore, and left. I didn't know who he was— a heavy man, clean-shaven. I could've just bought another copy, but this one was free.'

"Later, he told me he hadn't felt right that evening or during the night at the hotel. I didn't think much of it then, but now it all adds up. Not long after, John was sorting through his programs to have them bound together, and in that particular one, he found a strange piece of paper. It had red and black writing on it—very neat, and it looked like old symbols, almost like runes. He said, 'This must belong to that man at the concert. It looks important—maybe a copy of something. Someone put a lot of work into this. I wonder how I can return it.'

"We talked about it and decided it wasn't worth placing an ad. He said he'd just keep an eye out for the man at the next concert. The paper was sitting on a book by the fire—it was a chilly summer night. I think the door opened, though I didn't notice, and suddenly a warm breeze came between us and blew the paper into the fire. It was thin, and it burned up in a second. I said, 'Well, now you can't return it.' He didn't answer right away, then snapped, 'No, I can't—but I don't see why you keep saying that.' I told him I only said it once. 'No, you said it four times,' he replied. I remember that moment very clearly.

"Anyway, after John died, I reread Karswell's book. It was just as badly written as before—filled with grammar errors and sloppy ideas. He mixed myths, ancient legends, and even modern rituals in a confusing way. He treated everything like it was equally true, which made no sense. But this time, something felt different. One chapter especially caught my attention. It talked about 'casting the runes'—using them to charm someone or to get rid of them. The way he described it made me think he really believed it, maybe even practiced it. I now strongly suspect that the polite man at the concert was Karswell. I think that paper was extremely important. If John had been able to return it, maybe he wouldn't have died.

"So now I have to ask—do you have anything similar to add?"

In response, Dunning described what had happened at the British Museum when Karswell had returned his papers.

"So he actually gave you something," Harrington said. "Have you looked through the papers? No? Then we must do it right away."

They went to Dunning's house, which was still empty since his housekeeper and maid hadn't returned. On his writing desk, Dunning's portfolio sat untouched. He opened it and pulled out the stack of paper he used for note-taking. As he lifted it, a strip of very thin paper slipped out and fluttered across the room.

The window was open, but Harrington quickly slammed it shut and caught the paper just in time.

"I thought so," he said. "This could be the exact same kind of paper my brother found. You need to be very careful, Dunning. This could be a serious threat."

They talked for a long time. The strange paper was carefully examined. As Harrington had guessed, the symbols looked like runes, but neither of them could read or understand them. Both were nervous about copying the markings, afraid they might accidentally keep whatever curse or danger the paper carried alive. Because of this, no one has ever been able to figure out exactly what the paper said. But both Dunning and Harrington were sure that just owning it brought dangerous consequences. They agreed the paper had to be returned to the person who gave it, and the only safe way to do that was to hand it over directly. That wouldn't be easy, since Karswell already knew what Dunning looked like. Dunning would have to change his appearance—shaving his beard, for a start.

Still, they worried that something bad might happen before they could act. Harrington thought they might be able to predict the timing. He remembered that the concert where his brother got the cursed paper had taken place on June 18th, and his brother died exactly three months later, on September 18th. Dunning added that the writing he saw on the tram also mentioned "three months." With a nervous laugh, he said, "Maybe my time runs out in three months too." He checked his diary and found the date he was handed the paper— April 23rd. That meant his deadline was likely July 23rd.

"Now it's really important for me to know what happened to your brother during those last months," Dunning said.

"Of course," Harrington answered. "The worst thing for John was the feeling of constantly being watched when he was alone. Eventually, I started sleeping in his room, and that helped a bit. Still, he would talk in his sleep a lot. What he said wasn't always clear, and I don't know if it's a good idea to bring it all up right now. But I can tell you this: he got two strange items in the mail during that time. Both were sent from London, written in plain handwriting. One was an old woodcut from Bewick's collection—it showed a man walking down a moonlit road with a horrible creature following him. Someone had written lines from The Rime of the Ancient Mariner under it:

He keeps walking,

And doesn't look back,

Because he knows a terrifying creature

Is right behind him, following closely.

"The second was just a calendar, like the ones shops give out. John ignored it, but after he died, I noticed something—everything after September 18 had been torn out. You might wonder why he went out alone the night he died, but the strange thing is that in the last ten days of his life, he stopped feeling like he was being followed."

They ended their discussion with a plan. Harrington, who knew someone living near Karswell, thought he could find a way to track his movements. Dunning's job would be to stay ready to cross paths with Karswell and carry the paper in a place where he could easily reach it.

They parted ways. The following weeks were extremely stressful for Dunning. That invisible pressure that had started when he first got the paper now felt like a heavy shadow surrounding him. It kept him from thinking clearly or finding a way out. There was no one around to help, and he felt too drained to help himself. As May turned into June and then July, he waited in fear for Harrington's signal.

Finally, less than a week before the date Dunning feared most, he received a telegram:

"Leaves Victoria by boat train Thursday night. Do not miss. I come to you to-night. —Harrington."

Harrington arrived that night, and together they made their final plans. The train was set to leave Victoria Station at 9:00 p.m., with its last stop before Dover at Croydon West. Harrington would follow Karswell at Victoria Station and then watch for Dunning at Croydon. If necessary, he would call out using a fake name they had agreed on. Dunning, in disguise, would carry no luggage with his name or initials on it. Most importantly, he had to keep the paper close and ready.

Dunning waited nervously at the Croydon train platform. He had felt uneasy for weeks, and the feeling had only grown stronger. Strangely, things had felt calmer lately, but that only made him more worried—it seemed like a bad sign. If Karswell slipped away now, all hope might be lost. So many things could go wrong. Maybe this whole trip had been a trick. The twenty minutes he spent walking up and down the platform and asking every porter about the boat train were some of the most stressful moments he had ever experienced.

At last, the train arrived. Harrington was inside, looking out from a window. Dunning got on at the far end of the corridor so Karswell wouldn't recognize him, and slowly made his way to the right compartment. He was relieved to see that the train wasn't crowded.

Karswell seemed alert, but didn't seem to notice him. Dunning took a seat near him, trying to figure out how he might return the cursed paper without being noticed. Across from Karswell and next to Dunning was a pile of Karswell's coats. Slipping the paper into those wouldn't work—it had to look like Karswell accepted it himself. There was an open bag with papers inside. Maybe Dunning could hide the paper in it, and hope Karswell would forget the bag. Then, if Dunning handed it to him, that might count.

Several times Karswell left the compartment, and once Dunning almost made a move—but caught a warning glance from Harrington. Karswell was likely testing them, trying to see if they knew each other. He came back but didn't sit still for long. The third time he left, something fell from his seat to the floor. Karswell didn't notice and walked out of sight.

Dunning picked it up—it was one of those travel ticket cases with papers inside. Perfect. It had a pocket. He slipped the cursed paper into it just as Harrington stepped into the doorway and pretended to adjust the blind, helping to cover the action. They had timed it perfectly—the train was slowing down for Dover.

Karswell returned. Dunning, managing to keep his voice steady, held out the case. "May I give you this, sir? I think it's yours." Karswell checked it and replied, "Yes, it is. Much obliged," putting it into his coat pocket.

The next few moments were tense. The air in the carriage felt darker and warmer. Karswell looked uncomfortable, even scared. He pulled his coats close, then pushed them away, like something was wrong with them. He glanced nervously at Dunning and Harrington, and seemed about to speak when the train stopped at Dover Town.

It was a short ride to the pier, so the two men stepped out into the corridor. Once on the platform, they waited until Karswell passed by with his porter before quietly shaking hands and exchanging a few words of relief. Dunning nearly fainted from the stress, and Harrington helped steady him against a wall.

Harrington walked a little ahead to watch as Karswell boarded the ship. The ticket-taker looked at Karswell's ticket and let him pass, but then called out, "Sir, did the other gentleman show his ticket?" Karswell snapped back, "What are you talking about? What other gentleman?" The man leaned over to look at him and muttered, "Well, I don't know. My mistake—must've been your coats." Then, to a coworker nearby, he added, "Did he have a dog or something? Funny—I could've sworn he wasn't alone."

The boat pulled away. Soon, there was nothing to see but the ship's lights getting smaller, the line of Dover's lamps, the night wind, and the moon.

Back in their room at the "Lord Warden" hotel, Harrington and Dunning sat together in silence. Even though the danger seemed to be over, they were deeply troubled. Had they really sent someone to his death? Should they have warned him?

"No," said Harrington. "If he really did kill your brother, we did the right thing. But... maybe you should still try to warn him."

"He was only traveling to Abbeville," said Dunning. "I saw it on his ticket. I could send a message to the hotels there—something like 'Check your ticket case. —Dunning.' That might make me feel a little better.

Today's the 21st—he'd still have time. But I think it's too late. I think he's gone into the dark."

They sent the telegrams from the hotel just in case.

No one knows if Karswell ever got the messages or understood them. What is known is this: on the afternoon of July 23rd, an English traveler was standing outside St. Wulfram's Church in Abbeville, which was under repair. Suddenly, a stone fell from the scaffolding on the northwest tower and struck him on the head. He died instantly. No workers were on the scaffolding at the time. His papers identified him as Mr. Karswell.

One last note: At an auction of Karswell's belongings, Harrington bought a copy of Bewick's book. The page with the drawing of the traveler and the demon had been torn. And some time later, Harrington told Dunning a few things he had heard his brother mutter in his sleep—but Dunning quickly asked him to stop.

The End

Thank You for Reading

Dear Reader,

We hope this timeless classic has sparked your imagination and enriched your literary journey. Now that you've turned the final page, we want to share a vision for the future of reading—one where every classic you've ever wanted to explore is at your fingertips, in a format that best suits your life.

We'd like to invite you to gain immediate, unlimited digital & audiobook access to hundreds of the most treasured literary classics ever written—along with the option to secure deluxe paperback, hardcover & box set editions at printing cost. Together, we can spark a new global literary renaissance alongside our small, independent publishing house called "The Library of Alexandria."

Thousands of years ago, the Library of Alexandria stood as a beacon of knowledge—until it was lost to history. We aim to reignite that spirit of preservation and discovery right now, in the modern age—only this time, it's accessible to all, in every language and every format.

Picture a world where every timeless classic, novel, poem, or philosophical treatise is not only available to read but also updated for today's readers—modernized, translated into any language or dialect, and ready to enjoy in any format you choose, whether that is in an eBook, audiobook, paperback, or deluxe hardcover & box set version a printing cost.

By joining our movement to rebuild the modern Library of Alexandria, you become part of an unprecedented mission to offer:

- **Unlimited Audiobook & eBook Access to the Greatest Classics of All Time**

  Instantly explore thousands of legendary works, from Plato and Shakespeare to Jane Austen and Leo Tolstoy. All are instantly ready to read or listen to, giving you a complete literary universe at your fingertips.

- **Paperback & Deluxe Editions at Printing Costs:**

  Purchase any title in a paperback, deluxe hardbound, or deluxe boxset edition at printing costs, shipped right to your doorstep. Curate your personal library of Alexandria with editions worthy of display— crafted to last, designed to captivate, and delivered straight to your door.

- **Modern translations for Contemporary Readers in all languages and dialects**

  Discover a vast selection of classics reimagined in clear, current language—no more struggling with outdated phrases or obscure references. Next to the original versions, we aim to offer translations in as many languages and dialects as possible.

  As we continue our translation efforts and add new languages, readers everywhere can connect with these works as if they were written today. By bridging linguistic divides, you're contributing to ensuring that these timeless stories become more meaningful, accessible, and inspiring for people across the globe.

- **Your Personal Library of Alexandria:**

  Over the months and years, you'll curate a unique physical archive of classics—each volume a testament to your taste, curiosity, and love of knowledge. It's not just about owning books—it's about curating a cultural legacy you'll cherish and pass down for generations to come.

- **Join a Global Literary Renaissance:**

  Your support fuels an ongoing mission: allowing us to reinvest in offering deluxe print editions (including special boxsets) at their true cost, broaden the range of available formats and translations, and extend the reach of these works to new audiences worldwide. By joining today, you're not just preserving a legacy of masterpieces; you set in motion a powerful wave of literary accessibility.

We are more than a publisher—we're a movement, and we can't do it alone. Your support lets us scale our mission, preserving and reimagining history's greatest works for tomorrow's readers.

Become a Torchbearer of knowledge.

Thank you for picking up this book and allowing us into your literary journey. As you turn the pages, know that you're part of something larger: a global effort to keep these stories alive, share their wisdom across borders and generations, and spark a true cultural revival for the modern era.

If this resonates with you—please consider taking the next step by visiting:

www.libraryofalexandria.com

With gratitude and a shared love of knowledge,

The Modern Library of Alexandria Team

Visit:

www.libraryofalexandria.com

Or scan the code below:

www.ingramcontent.com/pod-product-compliance
Lightning Source LLC
Chambersburg PA
CBHW011526240626
47154CB00009B/2983